Schools Library and Information Services
S00000665656

Lenny's Lost Spots

First published in the UK in 2004 by
QED Publishing
A division of Quarto Publishing plc
The Fitzpatrick Building
188–194 York Way, London N7 9QP

A Catalogue record for this book is available from the British Library.

ISBN 1 84538 006 1

Written by Celia Warren
Designed by Alix Wood
Editor Hannah Ray
Illustrated by Genny Haines

Series Consultant Anne Faundez
Creative Director Louise Morley
Editorial Manager Jean Coppendale

Printed and bound in China

Lenny's Lost Spots

Celia Warren

QED Publishing

Lenny was a ladybird.
He was red with black spots.

In the morning Lenny counted his spots:
One, two, three, four, five, six.

But in the afternoon Lenny said,
“Where are my spots?
Where have they gone?
This morning I had six
and, now, I have none.”

Lenny looked once.
Lenny looked twice.
He thought his spots
were on some dice.
But he was wrong.

Lenny looked down.
Lenny looked up.
He thought his spots
were on a pup.
But he was wrong.

Lenny looked high.
Lenny looked low.
He thought his spots
were on a bow.
But he was wrong.

Lenny looked here.
Lenny looked there.
He thought his spots
were on a chair.
But he was wrong.

Lenny looked near.
Lenny looked far.
He thought his spots
were on a car.
But he was wrong.

Lenny looked left.
Lenny looked right.
He thought his spots
were on a kite.
But he was wrong.

Lenny went out in the rain.
He said, "My spots are back again."

And he was right.

What do you think?

What colour is Lenny?
What colour are his spots?

Can you count the
puppy's spots?

How did Lenny lose his spots?

Can you see
the spots in
this picture?
Are they
Lenny's spots?

Carers' and teachers' notes

- After reading and discussing the story, identify the rhymes and the refrain ('But he was wrong').
- Re-read the story, encouraging your child to join in with the rhyming words and the refrain.
- Count to six on your fingers. Then count Lenny's spots in the story. Give your child a ladybird template, made from card, with six legs and a red body. Provide your child with black paper spots and glue. Help your child to select six spots and to glue them in place. Count the spots, to reinforce the idea of the number six.
- Can your child remember an occasion when he/she was lost, or had lost something precious to him/her. How did he/she feel?
- Discuss who your child should safely approach if ever he/she is lost – consider different locations, e.g. in the supermarket, at the seaside, in the shopping precinct, etc.
- Collect pairs of opposites, beginning with the directions Lenny looked in the story (e.g. 'right'/ 'left', 'down'/'up'). Which words are not opposites? (E.g. 'once'/'twice'.)
- Fill a 'lost property' bag with tactile objects. Let your child dip into the 'feely' bag to see what he/she can find and identify by touch.
- Ask your child to draw a poster advertising a lost valuable or pet.
- Draw attention to the alliteration in the title of the story. Think of some other names beginning with 'L' that the ladybird might have had.
- Ask your child to retell the story in his/her own words.
- Look at the concepts of wet and dry using a sand tray. Encourage your child to experiment with water to wash sand off toys. What else do we use water for? E.g. to drink, to clean our teeth, to do the washing up, to have a bath.
- Find out more about the insect world and the real habitat of ladybirds. Where do they live? What do they eat? Do they always have six spots?